Through gates of unparalleled dream,
P'rea Press bids you a thousand welcomes.

I'm impressed. Kyla Ward's poetry is accessible, immediate, gripping. And she is bold enough to use traditional rhyme.

Peter Cannon, Senior Reviews Editor *Publishers Weekly* (NY), author *The Lovecraft Chronicles*, and *H. P. Lovecraft*

What a great collection, fantastically illustrated by the author. The first sections are a sort of call and response in iambic tetrameter, where you have Death on the one hand and the politician, the doctor, soldier and even the barista among the other. In every case, Death's message fits the subject. The last section of longer verse is steeped in myth and mythology, exquisitely rhymed.

A captive of iambic wiles,
Her verse enticed my thoughtful smiles.

Marge Simon, SFPA Grand Master, multiple SFPA Rhysling and HWA Bram Stoker awards winner

Kyla Lee Ward's poetic metre is as sharp as her indictments of the hypocrisies of the modern age. Equally at home examining the imagery of Michael Jackson's *Thriller* as she is contemplating mediæval depictions of the danse macabre, Ward accomplishes an alchemical marriage of the old and new to produce something which, like Death itself, transcends Time.

Adam Bolivar, author *The Lay of Old Hex*

With rapier-sharp poetics, Kyla Ward traipses through the graveyard on a macabre odyssey to illuminate, with charnel phosphorescence, the many pallid faces of death, as well as the mad grins of his myriad victims. Let her lead you, step by perilous step, on this imaginative and oft-times darkly comical Danse Macabre . . .

K. A. Opperman, author *The Crimson Tome*

Here is a shadowed and richly varied entertainment indeed! Whether updating the Danse Macabre with her own deftly crafted portraits, depicting the many faces of death in the world's mythologies, or proffering nuggets of weird scholarship, Kyla Lee Ward puts satisfying meat on the Gothic's bones. Her well-honed metrical and narrative skills, enhanced by a deep sense of history, make this collection a must for aficionados of literary dark verse.

Ann K. Schwader, multiple SFPA Rhysling winner and HWA Bram
Stoker awards nominee, author *Twisted in Dream, Dark Energies*

The Macabre Modern and Other Morbidities is deliciously elegant with a cloying side of Death. Dance into oblivion with the Burlesque Dancer or sleep to the notes of the Musician. Whatever your taste for the macabre, this collection has your flavor.

Ashley Dioses, author *Diary of a Sorceress*

Australian Shadows Award-winning poet Kyla Ward's flair for the mordantly macabre is uniquely her own; hers is a powerful voice in Australian poetic literature. Her spectral verse is vitally concerned with both life's pulsing rhythms and death's shadowy realms in this, her breathtaking new volume of *vers fantastique*. The poignant lines and piercing images of this collection will long haunt the sensitive reader.

Leigh Blackmore, author *Spores from Sharnoth and Other*
Madnesses, Horrors of Sherlock Holmes

In this new work, Kyla Ward brilliantly encapsulates the essence of existing Danse Macabre traditions, commenting on them and re-inventing them for the struggling world of the twenty-first century. With a wealth of humorous observation, grim whimsy, and ultimately life-confirming entertainment, it is a *memento mori* or even a Dante's *Inferno* for the twenty-first century—a guide to see us through to our inevitable end.

Robert Hood, multi-awarded horror writer, author *Peripheral Visions:*
The Collected Ghost Stories 1986–2015

With each new work she produces, Kyla Lee Ward—who, like William Blake and Clark Ashton Smith, has chosen to illustrate her own work—makes clear why she should be regarded as one of the preeminent exemplars of contemporary weird poetry. *The Macabre Modern and Other Morbidities* is a book to be savoured unhurriedly and with due contemplation of its essential message . . .

S. T. Joshi, award winning literary critic, author *I Am Providence,*
editor *Supernatural Literature of the World*

The Macabre Modern

THE MACABRE MODERN

AND OTHER MORBIDITIES

Kyla Lee Ward

Illustrated by Kyla Lee Ward
With an Introduction by Dr Gillian Polack
and an Afterword by S. T. Joshi
Edited by Charles Lovecraft

P'REA PRESS

Sydney, Australia
2019

KYLA LEE WARD is an Australian writer, actor and artist devoted to all things dark and beautiful. Her first poetry collection was *The Land of Bad Dreams* (P'rea Press 2011; reprinted 2016). Kyla's poetry has also appeared in *Abaddon, Avatars of Wizardry* (2012), *Bloodsongs, Gothic.Net, HWA Poetry Showcase V, Midnight Echo, Spectral Realms*, as well as in live performances. Her poem "Revenants of the Antipodes" (included in this collection) won the inaugural AHWA Australian Shadows Award for poetry 2018. Kyla's novel *Prismatic* (co-authored as "Edwina Grey") won the 2007 Aurealis Award for Best Horror. Her website is: www.kylaward.com

P'rea Press, Sydney Australia. Published August 2019.

Book designed by David E. Schultz.
Cover designed by David Schembri Studios.
Email: dschembristudios@gmail.com
Publisher's logo created by Charles Lovecraft.
Printed by Lightning Source Australia,
Unit A1/A3, 7 Janine St, Scoresby, Victoria 3179 Australia.
Set in Baskerville Old Face 11.5 point.

NATIONAL LIBRARY OF AUSTRALIA PREPUBLICATION DATA SERVICE ENTRY:
Author: Ward, Kyla.
Title: The Macabre Modern and Other Morbidities / Kyla Lee Ward;
Dr Gillian Polack; S. T. Joshi; Charles Alveric Lovecraft, editor.
ISBN: 978-0-9943901-2-7 (paperback)
Gothic poetry (Literary genre)
Australian poetry—21st century

Dedication

to my friends

What lies behind the mask
Is what all masks reveal,
And like a maze of mirrors
This secret sets its seal
Of fantasy, of deepest fear,
Or dark desire low,
And what you seek is what you find;
And now 'tis you should know
What lies behind the mask . . .

Contents

The Loquacious Cadaver

Lucubration

Afterword *by S. T. Joshi*

Illustrations

INTRODUCTION

Christianity was originally a cultus. Its members collected the bones of saints. In worshipping them, it celebrated Death. This led to many things, some of them sacred and holy and some of them . . . worrying.

What do people do when faced with the fear and the ludicrousness of their own past? What do they do when faced with the impossible contradictions in something so very close to home? A dramatic answer to these questions would make a wonderful sound bite, but it wouldn't explain Kyla Ward's *Macabre Modern*, a contemporary update on the medieval Danse Macabre theme.

The original danse macabre was a series of late medieval descriptions of images. It was a visual, visceral reaction to a world plagued by death. And Death, in this milieu, wasn't Terry Pratchett's curry-loving gentleman—a skeleton, a scythe, a symbol. A monstrous corpse, Death led the dead in a helpless, jerky dance.

In an earlier incarnation and under a different name Death led a fearsome hunt, with his entourage torturing souls along their road to doom. Hellequin's Hunt was a reason to stay in bed and not to wander the forest after dark. Each rider and walker in the Hunt was explained by the form of their punishment, and those punishments reflected their lives. Simple allegories to explain, darkly, that the pain individuals suffered on their way to Judgement was deserved. A black frisson of warning for the rest of us; a hell journey for the adulterer or liar.

Kyla Ward's *Macabre Modern* is not a simple updating of an old theme. Nor was the late medieval one a simple updating of the allegorical poems of the High Middle Ages. Both works tell us that Death waits for us all, while leaving us in the hope that our part in the dance may start late.

The form of this dance is similar to a Masque. It takes the Tudor and Stuart public performance and carries it to the present day. It adds the dark bite of Ben Jonson's combination of philosophy and politics in the body of characters in a play to the dancing skeletal Death of earlier eras. Each voice in Ward's *Modern* represents the world and comments on the world.

The form of this dance is similar to a Masque. It links Roman cultus to Jean Paul Sartre's *Huis Clos*. A room for eternity, where one is condemned always to be with those whom one cannot bear. Death triumphant and each soul facing him in his or her particular way.

The form of this dance is similar to a Masque. It uses a poetic form to argue deep truths about the human condition. The Word becomes the World, and warns us.

There are so many historical rituals and plays where humans face death. So very many. We need them all. That small bit of morbidity carried through from Early Christianity gave our culture (Christian and other) the need to solve problems: problems of death; problems of story; problems of self. This is what Ward's *Macabre Modern* is, using an old narrative form. Ward brings together so many incongruencies to create art.

This art is full of pain. This happens when one flirts with Death. The only way through pain for some of us is dark laughter and satire. Watch carefully, for when Death comes too close, the laughter proves to be rictus, and your straight back demonstrating your noble worth is nothing but rigor mortis. Then the pain turns into triumph, but the triumph is never ours.

Death wins. Always.

—Dr Gillian Polack

The Macabre Modern

The Authority Speaks

Such contemplative sorts who give
due thought to the best way to live
encounter, by design or chance,
a universal human dance,
commencing as the heartbeat halts,
which, rather like the bridal waltz,
may please the viewer or appal,
but surely will be done by all.

The Danse Macabre's initial scheme
was quite the medieval meme
and spread through Europe on the wing
of Gutenberg's great conjuring.
The present author, cognisant
of debt here owing to Marchant
and Lydgate, has reworked it some
to suit this new millennium.

MOVERS AND SHAKERS

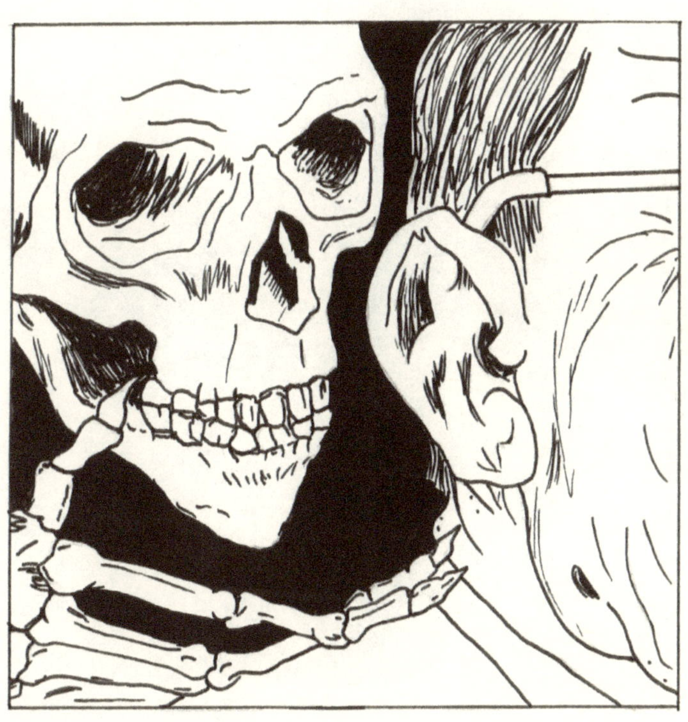

The Politician

DEATH

We share the democratic claim:
to us, all people are the same!
You stood before your peers and vowed
to be their voice and speak aloud
their wants and needs, and grace supply.
I need a partner: judging by
the principles which you rehearsed
it's fitting that you be the first!

THE POLITICIAN

I lead the dance? Oh goodness, no!
That stirring speech was all for show!
You do not comprehend the way
democracy exists today.
I represent my party's will
to power and our donors' bill.
Unhand me! I am not at all
responsible, nor can recall!

The C. E. O.

DEATH

Upon the glassine heights I see
an emperor of industry!
For governments may come and go
while companies contrive to grow.
I come a-knocking at the door
where wealth and power came before.
Necessity demands you die.
Alas! No benefits apply!

THE C. E. O.

You think that only you can bring
a radical restructuring?
I'd sever any neck but mine
in service of the bottom line!
I slashed the budget, trimmed the fat,
and drained their brains on top of that!
If this does not win your respect,
then go ahead and vivisect!

The Financier

DEATH

This one presents a classic case!
That belly and congested face
betray the inner void of greed:
you hoarded far beyond your need.
To mortgage, close, on-sell and seize
on privatised utilities
was all in vain! All you could pay
will not buy you another day!

THE FINANCIER

Now listen, you pathetic mime,
of course my money bought me time!
With private room and special care,
and kidneys sourced from who knows where!
If regulation I opposed
and there were dealings undisclosed,
a good return on what I spent
enables me to die content.

Icons

The Old Royal

DEATH

A sovereign's death was once announced
by comets, as the princes pounced
upon the title and domain.
It's good to be back here again!
Come take my hand, as darkness falls,
and process through these gilded halls
one final time; such natal chance
grants no advantage in the dance.

THE OLD ROYAL

This night was long in coming, yet
I leave the world with great regret,
suspecting I am not alone:
that with me dies the very throne!
The dignity which once adhered
to my estate has disappeared
with purpose, in this latter age,
a flower pressed in history's page.

The Celebrity

DEATH

A willing partner here at last!
Whose hand is smooth, whose step is fast.
Such earthly angels, once deceased,
routinely find their fame increased!
As amber, each iconic scene
preserves your carapace pristine.
Eternal glory somewhat flat,
but not a whit less real for that.

THE CELEBRITY

Your words should consolation bring;
and yet they have a hollow ring,
for moulded by a thousand hands
my guise but answered the demands
of press and public: all they see
is all the use they made of me,
their compliments like razors strewn
along the path I trod so soon.

The Athlete

DEATH

You built a life upon your first
achievement, not the best nor worst.
To stand, to walk, to jump and run:
each moment saw the last outdone!
You honed your body like a sword,
cut time and heard the world applaud.
You never turned from race or row.
Say then, why do you falter now?

THE ATHLETE

I quake, my last event declared,
to find myself so unprepared.
What regimen, what mental lash,
could fit me for this final dash?
Without my muscles, heart and veins,
and pumping lungs, all which remains
is but my will, a fragile thing!
Now I am done with practising.

PROFESSIONS

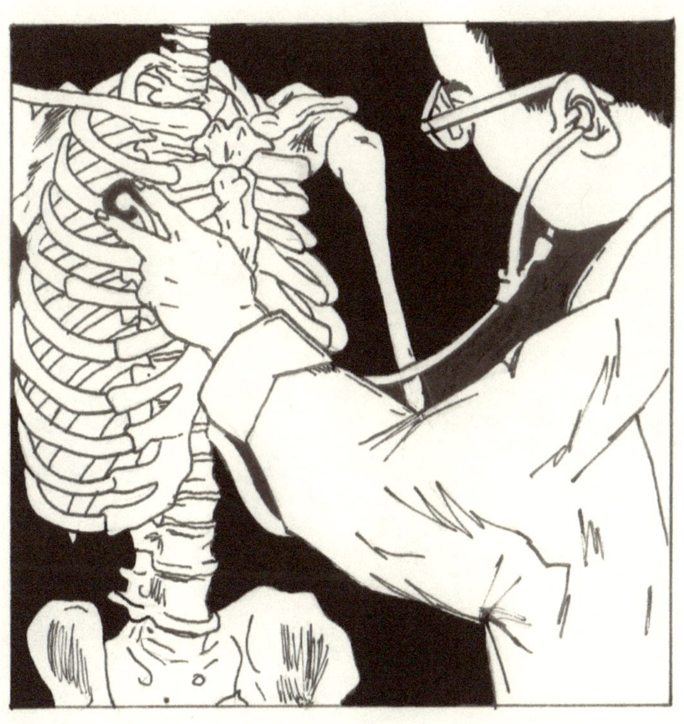

The Doctor

DEATH

How many times we two have crossed
the scythe with scalpel, won and lost.
I see you now sans cap and mask.
Old friend, it's time to leave your task
and join the ones you could not save
within the far from sterile grave.
But do not look so woebegone!
The ones you *did* will follow on!

THE DOCTOR

But death's inevitability
makes every day a victory!
And somewhere in my cooling brain
a sparking synapse must remain
to spin this whole balletic dream!
And when the paramedic team
adrenaline and shock apply,
I fear that I must say goodbye!

The Lawyer

DEATH

Concerns of justice set aside,
for misadventure, homicide,
and natural cause are all occult
when one considers the result!
And you who sought to fix the truth
shall hear it now: both age and youth
must join the dance, both rich and poor.
A truly universal law!

THE LAWYER

I'd argue definition here:
when death arrives is seldom clear!
Is this a vegetative state?
I must see the certificate!
Until the probate is released
no one is legally deceased.
You surely must retain your clerk:
at least *think* of the paperwork!

The Architect

Death and the Architect

No door will serve to keep me out.
Must I construct a grim redoubt
No wall yet raised will turn me back.
in fear of such profound attack?
No roof avails against my rain.
But I prefer a sweet domain
No dam repels my creeping tide.
with lawns and gardens spreading wide!
A narrow chamber I reveal,
In glass and marble, brick and steel,
with granite cap, and walled in pine.
I'll shape this place to my design
I'm sure that keeping this in mind
and know fulfilment of a kind,
would have been only provident.
contributing the fundament.

Follies

The Advertiser

DEATH

How many promises you made!
And you would seem to have betrayed
the vast majority: why should
what people think is bad or good,
or covet, change from year to year?
You dread no judgement, that is clear!
But tell me, do you see a trend
in humankind's communal end?

THE ADVERTISER

From costumed lynchings by the Klan
to hara-kiri in Japan,
you may view fashion with contempt,
but death itself is not exempt!
You might expand in time of war
but presently, I'm *very* sure,
a more exclusive service would
do your core brand the world of good.

The Life Coach

DEATH

Upon a time, the wise would mull
their problems over on a skull.
No such memento here, I see:
perhaps you weren't expecting me?
In death, your worries culminate,
resolving in a simpler state:
a fact you surely should address
when cultivating mindfulness.

THE LIFE COACH

This "death" advice you seek to give
could be a bit more positive!
Our dreams die if we don't rebel
and lacking love, we might as well.
We die inside to be reborn,
but you come on so pale and wan,
it undercuts the whole routine!
My time is up? What do you mean?

The Manager

DEATH

I feel a twinge of sympathy
at how confused you seem to be.
A pear, a shoe, a book, a knife,
a bar of gold, a human life,
are all distinct in form and name,
and yet you treat them all the same!
No question that your work is through,
but what exactly did you do?

THE MANAGER

I *managed*, don't you understand?
You can't believe I worked by hand
or harvested, or took a tithe:
whatever you do with that scythe!
You can't blame me for what occurred
to all the units I transferred
or dropped. But how can I protest?
I'm worth no more than all the rest.

VOCATIONS

The Soldier

DEATH

The glorious martial enterprise
demands each soldier kills or dies.
No matter where the conflict lies,
no veteran this truth denies!
For they have heard the feeble cries
emerging from beneath the flies.
So, gazing in your swollen eyes,
why do I see such shocked surprise?

THE SOLDIER

They said that in the drone brigade
there was no need to be afraid,
so at my console fast I stayed
and you can see the price I paid!
If I had faced a gun or blade
instead of what my screen displayed,
then less surprised, though still dismayed,
I'd join this passing-out parade.

The Farmer

DEATH

You reap your harvest when it's due:
how much the better cropper you!
Though we equip ourselves alike,
I spare no season from my strike.
You need no tutelage to see
life's basic circularity,
or know the worth, past that of oil,
of deep and rich, composted soil.

THE FARMER

In fact, I've been expecting you:
the powers-that-be oblige me to
deploy so many kinds of 'cide
that human life can scarce abide!
And though I welcome this release,
I doubt you bring me lasting peace.
I'll walk a spectre, in whose lee
the food chain rattles dolefully.

The Teacher

DEATH

Of all the things that lie beyond
my reach, I praise the sacred bond
of knowledge passed from old to young.
To you have generations clung!
You gave them language, kindled dreams,
revealed the world's recurrent themes,
and even in your sleep shall know
respect of those you helped to grow.

THE TEACHER

Life's lesson learned, I gladly go
to take what rest I may below.
But thanks of *them?* Don't make me laugh!
For comprehension, speech and math-
ematics hold no weight today.
If they recalled a single way
their mind's estate could be increased,
they might respect themselves, at least.

CREATIVES

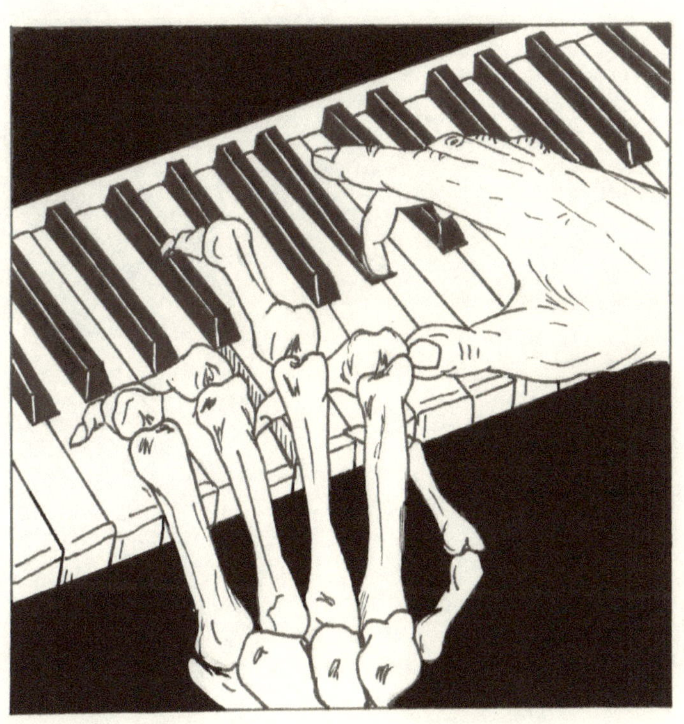

The Musician

DEATH

Sweet David, we have met before,
but now there can be no encore,
nor backing save a failing heart
which beats to tear the world apart.
Yet, even as I draw you near,
what is this music that we hear?
That snares us on its subtle barb,
the music of the danse macabre.

THE MUSICIAN

Dear friend, I know the answer well:
it is my own! And more to tell,
all ballads that were ever made
and pieces that were ever played
pass influences forward, back,
a phrase, a riff, a theme, a track.
All echo through eternity,
the music of humanity.

The Programmer

Death

Such minds as find the world unsafe
in mathematics place their faith
and as philosophers of old
take comfort in proportions gold.
I understand your need to reach
beyond the great conceptual breach:
but one more step and you shall see
both zero and infinity!

The Programmer

There's so much that you just don't *get*
about computers and the net!
Through calculations so diverse,
I built a second universe
where lightning leaps from node to node!
And had I managed to upload
my consciousness into the cloud,
your presence had been disallowed!

The Artist

DEATH

Between the pencil and the ink,
the hammer-fall and chisel-clink,
the artist, when her time is through,
must cease her work like any crew.
This deadline genius cannot cheat:
the opus you leave incomplete
will stand, as if some cruel Divine
meant this imperfect world a sign.

THE ARTIST

This world reserves, when all is said,
its plaudits for the artist dead.
When I am gone, they'll say how I
did suffer, struggle, starve, and sigh:
through very passion met decease!
And even an unfinished piece
will gain in value, guaranteed!
Come, partner, you may take the lead!

THE SMALL JOBS

The Office Worker

DEATH

How very odd this complex seems!
A cleanly dungeon, lacking screams,
which even those who mortify
themselves for God do not deny.
And you, the inmate, lacking chains:
do I release you from your pains
or tear you from epiphany?
Come, carcass, stir, and answer me!

THE OFFICE WORKER

How did the hours slip away?
There were some bills I had to pay
and then my rental grew so dear . . .
I never thought I'd still be here
when came the end! So many dreams,
all buried now, beneath the reams
of copying. For all I do
I might as well come dance with you.

The Barista

DEATH

To feed a family, keep a home
on nothing more than beans and foam,
may be accounted as a feat,
but do you think your life complete?
If you had dreamed of doing more
upon this earth, that time is o'er.
The draught from the espresso bar,
alas! is not ambrosia.

THE BARISTA

It's easy come and easy go!
By far the finest life I know
is one of honest expertise,
and serving people as they please.
Though I might not have made a splash,
I still retain sufficient dash
to demonstrate my special knack:
somehow, I think you take it black!

The Taxi Driver

DEATH

Where to? Where to? The dying ask.
To answer that is not my task.
I merely bear them through the door
where all their kin have gone before
and in that time, when folk were wise,
the dead wore coins upon their eyes.
But though I take no less a care,
these days I do not charge a fare.

THE TAXi DRIVER

Sure, have a laugh at my expense!
Not all receive the recompense
that's due to years of driving hard,
enduring scorn and disregard.
Should I think you my rescuer
for making me the passenger?
I'll ask "Where to?" If you don't know,
I'll gladly tell you where to go!

THE DEMIMONDE

The Burlesque Dancer

Death

Come, take the floor with me, my dear!
Though multitudes would call you dear,
the gifts I bring may yet endear
me closer to your heart, my dear.
And though this dance may cost you dear
in leaving all that you hold dear,
the silence and the darkness, dear,
will keep you soft and close, and dear.

The Burlesque Artist

If come you to pronounce my doom,
then don't try to disguise the doom
to which birth does us all foredoom!
I danced in knowledge of my doom
each night upon the stage, a doom-
sayer that dressed in red. This doom
adds piquancy to life. No doom
compares to an undying doom!

The Drug-Dealer

DEATH

There's some would say you courted me.
I fear that I must disagree!
You might have chivvied souls my way,
but that was so you'd eat this day.
You might have claimed you didn't care
to make your enemies beware,
but loved your life enough to do
what few would have the stomach to.

THE DRUG-DEALER

I always thought my death would be
the picture of futility:
a slumping posture of defence.
I never dreamed that you'd make sense!
Though I may fall, some other kid
will rise to fill the place I did.
He'll be the city's darker teat,
and nature's cycle shall complete.

The Activist

DEATH

So many people scarcely pause,
but die for any kind of cause.
To live for one's another thing:
your tolerance for suffering
must be at once extreme and nil!
But now your dream I shall fulfil.
All classes are alike to me,
the only true equality!

THE ACTIVIST

And so I die: too soon to see
the changes which might come to be.
Too late to spare myself the pain
of wondering if I fought in vain.
If all I did was all I could,
yet not enough, was it still good?
Was it still right? The secret doubt
of all my days must now come out!

LIFE STAGES

The Pensioner

DEATH

So long, so long you've made me wait,
the song has changed, the desolate
expanse of floor where couples twined
intimidates, but calm your mind.
I care not if your sight is poor
or that your step has grown unsure.
All you have lost to circumstance
shall be no hindrance in the dance.

THE PENSIONER

My breath may catch, my limbs may shake:
you're not the partner I would take!
Although there's much that I forget,
a love of living lingers yet.
It is the *world* that has decayed,
which spins confused and all afraid.
And seated here, I am still me:
are you the only one to see?

The Adolescent

DEATH

A noose attached, a footstool cast:
you dance the jig of those who passed
when life was an incoming tide,
too strong, it seems, for all to ride.
It might have been the only way
you felt events could end today,
but what tomorrow might have brought
had merited a second thought.

THE ADOLESCENT

You say that I have done and been?
This isn't *fair:* I didn't mean
to really die, just stop a while
and find myself a better style.
You're just like all the people who
don't understand or bother to:
I bet you think I'm really dumb!
Why didn't anybody come?

The Child

DEATH

Oh, baby blue and baby pink,
what brings you here I cannot think!
Despite all legislative care
and medical, attention, prayer,
you join the dance! At penalty
of all you were supposed to be.
Whatever will your parents do,
O baby pink and baby blue?

THE CHILD

Godfather black, godmother white,
don't aggravate my parents' plight!
For all the things I might have been
at best were visions dimly seen.
My future always was my own,
its challenges to face alone.
Their love accompanies me back,
godmother white, godfather black!

CONCEPTS

The Death of the Author

The semiotician Roland Barthes
sought to refresh the critic's art
when he, in sixty-seven, wrote
a "text is a tissue of quot-
ations." In short, an author was
much more of an effect than cause.
The fact remains, each book is writ
by one whose expertise and wit,
or lack thereof, brings it to be.
The author is not dead, but she
is harried by a strange brigade
insisting she need not be paid
for all the energy and time
it takes to forge a proper rhyme!
As Barthes himself would surely say,
we see disturbing signs today.

The End of History

In 'eighty-nine, the Berlin Wall
(in place of nukes) began to fall
and Francis Fukuyama penned
that history had reached its end
and liberal democracy
throughout the world would come to be
(though not without the odd Event)
the final form of government.
The intervening years have seen
some bankers exercise their lien,
dictators here and there deceased,
surveillance everywhere increased
and definitions of that state
(to which we surely all relate)
have stretched so far, no trick to tell
that history's alive and well!

The Sixth Extinction

There came a fall of meteorites
and everything from ammonites
to archosaurs failed to survive:
that was extinction number five.
The victims of the sixth include
the mammoth and the dodo's brood.
It's happening as you read this verse,
and signs are that it's getting worse;
but scientists declaiming that
endanger their own habitat.
That temperatures shall only climb
and that we're losing plants this time
are both dismissed as false alarms
by those whose factories, mines, and farms
lie at the root of all this ruin.
Why do we think that we're immune?

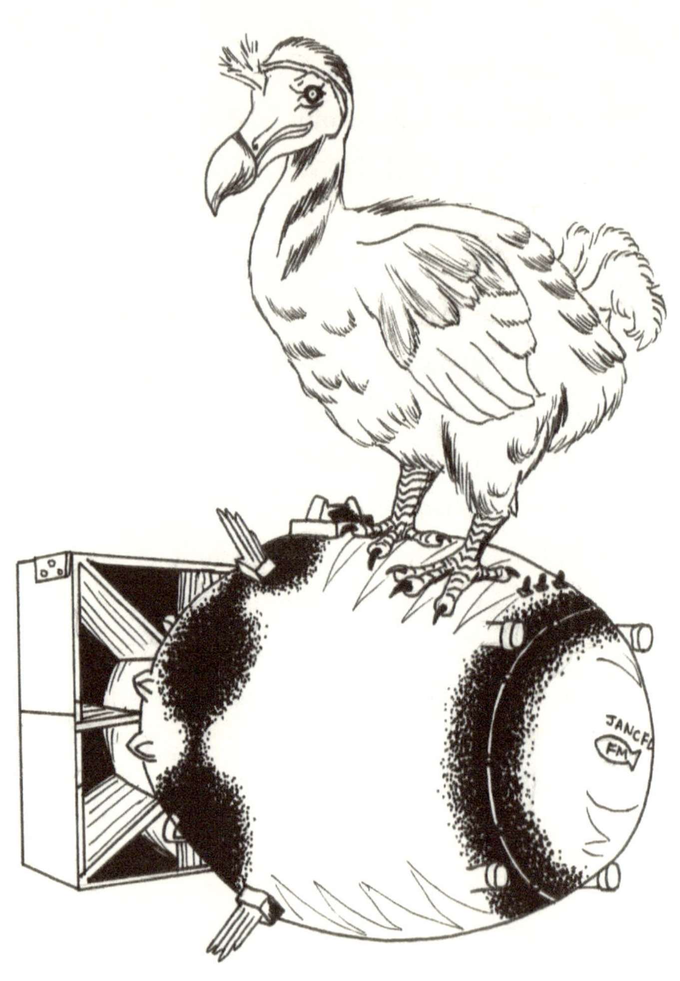
JANCF
FM

The Authority Concludes

As humans we can comprehend
the vulgar insult of our end.
We may see less decay and blight
than did the average Saxon wight;
and yet the need to make some sense
of death remains, despite pretence,
that with the right gym membership
we will escape its bony grip.

This Danse Macabre strays from its source,
omitting feudal rank, of course,
and granting humankind the sway
to bring about Earth's final day.
But this remains: all that you do
sends consequences marching through.
Disclaim intent or call it chance,
but how you live is how you dance.

The Danse Macabre

an essay

"You might be a king or a little street sweeper, but sooner or later you dance with the reaper."

—Death, in Bill and Ted's Bogus Journey,
written by Chris Matheson and Ed Solomon, directed by Peter
Hewitt (Nelson Entertainment et al., 1991)

What exactly is a danse macabre?

The word macabre makes its first known appearance in the fourteenth century poem, "Respit de la Mort" ("Respite from Death") by the French poet Jean Le Fevre. The line reads, "Je fis de macabre la dance" (roughly, "I did the macabre dance"). The context suggests that this qualifies the poet to pronounce on the ubiquity of death, the fate that ultimately awaits all who are born. Some commentators think Le Fevre must have narrowly escaped dying through accident or disease, and distilled the experience into this work. But why did he describe it as a dance?

According to the current Oxford English Dictionary, macabre means "disturbing because concerned with or causing a fear of death." This makes "macabre" a remarkably consistent word, for one that has migrated from French to English (and the Italian "macabro") and is still in use after seven hundred years. Certain contemporary Western symbols of death and the dead do derive from medieval Europe, though seldom directly. Consider the personification of death as a scythe-wielding, black-cowled skeleton. "There's a Mr Grim here, he's come about the reaping" (*The Meaning of Life*, written by Monty Python, directed by Terry Gilliam [Universal Pictures et al., 1983]). A scythe is carried by a black-veiled woman with bat wings in the fresco *The Triumph of Death*, painted by Buonamico Buffalmacco in the Camposanto Monumentale in Pisa (somewhere between 1336 and 1341 C. E. and recently restored). But, although intimidating, she is very far from skeletal. The death which joins its fellow horsemen of the apocalypse in the anonymous folio CCCCCLXXVII recto in the Bible, vol. 2, Nuremberg (1478), carries a scythe but also a sword. It is skeletal, but stark naked. In the 1494 painting *Death of the Miser* by Hieronymus Bosch, death comes in the form of a withered corpse, draped not in black but in white. A black cowl is worn by the demonic figure at the foot of the bed.

These days, a white-draped figure is coded as a ghost. "If you are real ghosts, you guys better get another routine because those sheets, they don't work," says Lydia in *Beetlejuice* (written and directed by Tim Burton [Geffen Co., 1988]). Not when they're floral print, perhaps, but the medieval dead were wrapped or sewn into large pieces of white cloth, called shrouds. Both clothes and coffins were expensive, so most corpses were simply enshrouded and lowered into the grave. Medieval or Renaissance depictions of actual ghosts are thin on the ground, but, in the fifteenth-century depiction of the Witch of Endor by the Master of Otto van Moerdrecht, the apparition of Samuel rises draped in white (and truth be told, looks rather Grecian).

However, jumping back to *Beetlejuice*, young Lydia continues her interrogation of the hapless Maitlands, displaying what might be considered a macabre curiosity. "I'm not scared of sheets. Are you gross under there? Are you *Night of the Living Dead* under there? Like all bloody veins and pus?"

In every era, every society finds its own way of dealing with death. The urge to depict and interrogate jostles with the urge to distance oneself from unpleasantness. Outbreaks of the Black Death during the fourteenth and fifteenth centuries sparked a wave of macabre usages. The advances in medicine and increase in personal wealth experienced in the West during the twentieth century incline us towards distance, after the unprecedented carnage of two world wars. But there have been reactions; there has been, in recent decades, a macabre curiosity.

We cannot access the actual experience of people living in the Middle Ages, but we may contemplate the *memento mori*, "Remember, thou too shalt die." This was what everyone, from prince to peasant, was advised to do by the Christian church. Contemplating the inevitability of death was presented as an antidote to sin. Why risk your immortal soul for things that would pass as swiftly as your own life?

The legend of the three living and the three dead men is

recounted many times during the period, notably by the French poet Baudoin de Condé in a manuscript dated to the thirteenth century. Three men of high rank are out hunting when they encounter three animate and quite articulate corpses, who point out that they were once just like them. Geoffrey Chaucer, writing between 1387 and 1400, provides a variation in *The Pardoner's Tale*, in which three drunken young men accost a stranger on the road, demanding the location of "A certain traitor Death, who singles out, and kills the fine young fellows here about." Really, they should have known better than to ask directions of a strange, pale figure, all wrapped up except the face!

The danse macabre conducted by Jean le Fevre and so many after him likens death to a village dance, one of the chain dances that continually picks up new participants behind the leader. The metaphor was not limited to this usage: a person executed on the gallows was said to dance, as were victims of the bite of a tarantula. The Spanish dance called the Tarantella is supposedly based on their spasms. But during the Medieval and Renaissance periods (though later incidents are recorded) the link was incarnate in outbreaks of the so-called dancing mania.

Tradition places the first incident in the year 1021 (some accounts 1027) in the German village of Kolbig, and describes it as a curse pronounced by the local priest on people who missed mass to go dancing. In the year 1278, in Utrecht, two hundred people are said to have spontaneously begun dancing on the Mosel Bridge. As a result, it collapsed, plunging all to their deaths.

In 1374, in the town of Aachen (modern Aix-la-Chapelle), up to four hundred residents began dancing in the streets, hand in hand in what was described as a wild delirium, and continued without eating or drinking until they collapsed with exhaustion. Some died outright and others never completely recovered. According to J. F. C. Hecker's *The Black Death and the Dancing Mania* (translated from the German by B. G. Babbington [Cassell, 1888]—although uncited, his source appears to be the records of the town council), some who did recover afterwards asserted that they felt as if they had been immersed in a stream of blood, which obliged them to leap so high. Over the next four years the phenomenon spread, like the plague, to Cologne and thence from town to town down the Rhine valley and across what is now southern France. Another severe outbreak commenced in Strasbourg in 1418.

In the 1520s, the doctor and alchemist known as Paracelsus put forward the theory that this *choreomania* was a kind of contagious idea (in a tract titled *The Diseases That Deprive Man of His Reason*). Many modern commentators follow him in considering it a response, in a tightly knit community, to deadly assaults upon that community, such as plague, flood, or other catastrophe. Again, it is not a mind-set that most of us can directly access. Nor is there any way to draw a direct link between any of these potential inspirations and the danse macabre. What we do know is that, somewhere in or around 1425, an anonymous artist produced a fresco of animate, articulate corpses drawing monk, craftsman, and labourer, but also pope, king, and knight into the dance, on the walls of le Cimetière des Innocents in Paris. Much has been written about the Cemetery of the Innocents; how markets and open-air sermons, even festivals, were held before the porticoes in which were piled the disordered bones of those whose time in the sacred earth was up. A great statue of Death in partially skeletal form overlooked proceedings: it is now in the Louvre, the only part of the fittings to have survived, apart from such bones as were moved to the Paris catacombs.

The likely form of these frescoes and the text of the verses accompanying them are known to us through manuscript copies and a book of woodcut prints published in 1485 by the Parisian printer Guyot Marchant. These copied the frescoes and transcribed the verses that ran beneath them, and were a runaway success. So much so that Marchant commissioned a sequel, with original art and new verses by the fashionable poet Martial d'Auvergne, which was published in 1486. The original dance listed thirty ranks and occupations of men. The sequel attempted to do the same with women. D'Auvergne's danse features the Queen and the Abbess, and creates wives for various worthies such as the Knight and the Merchant. His actual female occupations, however, are a fascinating list, including Theologianess, Housekeeper, Chamber

Maid, Nun, Shepherdess, Midwife, Wet-nurse, and Witch, and ending (in the second edition of 1491) with a female Fool.

The Death in these woodcuts is indeed a corpse. Although it has some skeletal aspects, it retains lank hair and a withered musculature. In some pictures, the gaping hole in its abdomen shows where the guts have exploded. But as corpses go, this one is particularly lively! Here flinging back its shroud and tripping a lively measure, here dragging its partner along and laughing all the while. For all ranks and both sexes, the verses are in the form of a dialogue, with Death addressing the victim, who responds. Here I have recourse to the English translation made by the monk John Lydgate, who upon returning from a trip to Paris in 1426 is said to have copied both the pictures and verses of the men's dance onto the walls of the cloister of St Paul's Cathedral, adding a Princess and an Abbess for good measure. Again, the original is long destroyed, but copies exist in manuscript and a printed edition of 1554.

Lydgate's verses present suitably sombre warnings and pious wishes. Death acknowledges the Pope as Christ's representative on earth, but "Vp-on this daunce / [ʒe] firste begyn shal / As moste worthi lorde" ("Upon this dance you first shall begin, as most worthy lord"). The Pope responds, "For whiche al honoure / who prudentely can see / Is litel worthe / that doth soo sone pace" ("For which all honour, the prudent may see, is of little worth that so soon passes"). Death advises the Princess that all her dignity and accomplishments grant her no consideration, prompting her to observe that "Dethe hathe yn erthe / no ladi ne maiestresse" ("Death has on earth no lady or mistress"—and thus cannot be expected to behave chivalrously).

But the verses are also frequently comic. In its speech to the Abbot, Death notes his massive stomach. "ʒe mote come daunce / thowʒ ʒe be nothing light" ("You must come dance, though you be nothing light"). Furthermore, "Who that is fattest / I haue hym be-hight / In his graue / shal sonnest putrefie" ("The fattest man, I promise, in his grave shall be the first to rot"). Death mocks the physician for spending his life examining urine and points out that it is a good "leech" who can heal himself. But some of the dancers give as good as they get: the minstrel criticises "This newe daunce" for its dreadful footing and inconsistent measure.

John Lydgate was not the only tourist to take inspiration from the mural at des Innocents. The French town of Auvergne created their own version in the Chaise-Dieu, depicting Death playing the bagpipes as well as dancing. In the church of Täby in Sweden, it actually does play chess. In 1440, a danse was rendered on the exterior wall of the cathedral in Basel, Switzerland. In 1463, another was added to St Mary's Church in Lübeck, Germany, followed closely by another in Tallinn, Estonia. In addition to this, on at least one occasion the danse was adapted into a masque. This was performed at night in the palace of the Duc de Burgundy in 1449, by the light of standing candelabras.

The tale of "Hopfrog" by Edgar Allan Poe is incontestably derived from a tale concerning a medieval French King—the "Bal des Ardents" of Charles the Mad. In 1842, the same author wrote "The Masque of the Red Death." Again, there is no demonstrable link, yet what do we have here? An uninvited guest, arrayed as the corpse of a plague victim, whose progress through the ball heralds the death of all present. In any case, 1842 is getting thoroughly ahead of ourselves.

In 1538, the well-known painter Hans Holbein the Younger reinterpreted the now hundred-year-old trope, releasing his own set of woodcuts, with verses by the French poet Gilles Corrozet and an introduction by the theological author Jean de Vauzèlles. They are conceivably based upon the danse in his adopted home of Basel, yet very much a creation of their time.

The quality and detail in these prints are astounding. Marchant's pictures are lively and charming, but these are masterpieces. Here we do encounter the familiar, comparatively hygienic skeleton, stealing the crown from the emperor, running the knight through with his own lance, and adorning the countess with a necklace made of bones. The image of it climbing out of the waves that endanger a ship is astounding, and the one where it leads the child away from sobbing parents is heart-rending.

The text also differs significantly. "The images of death are the true and proper mirror by which one must correct the deformities of sin and embellish the soul," writes de Vauzèlles, which is traditional enough. But there is no dialogue here between Death and victim; the short quatrains are blunt in their meaning and each is prefaced by two biblical quotations. And the respect granted the Pope and the joke played on the Abbot in the fifteenth century become brutal attacks in the sixteenth. In 1517, an argumentative monk had nailed his critique of the papacy to a cathedral door in a town quite near to Basel, and by 1538 the bloodthirsty struggle for land and souls that would become known as the Reformation was in full swing. Is it coincidence that one of the largest recorded outbreaks of the dancing mania occurred in Strasbourg in 1518, followed by Basel itself in 1536?

In 1785, on the eve of their own bloody revolution, the officials of Paris ordered the closure of des Innocents, and all remains interred there were moved to the tunnels of an old marble quarry. As said, the original mural was long gone and most of its imitators had also succumbed by this time to weathering and metaphors more genteel than a bagpipe-playing, chain-dancing corpse. A fragment of the Tallinn mural does survive, to this day.

But does the symbol? There are millennial reapers and ghosts in sheets, but has the danse itself made it this far?

In order to answer this question, we must first consider the *Danse Macabre* of French composer Camille Saint-Saëns. This is a "tone poem" for orchestra, written in 1874. It started out as a song based on a poem by the Symbolist Henri Cazalis:

> Zig, zig, zig, Death in cadence,
>
> Striking with his heel a tomb,
>
> Death at midnight plays a dance-tune,
>
> Zig, zig, zig, on his violin . . .

In answer to these summons, the dead (described as "white skeletons . . . running and leaping in their shrouds") rise from their graves and dance till cockcrow announces dawn, whereupon they retreat once more to the shadows. This program is followed faithfully by Saint-Saëns, incorporating xylophones to suggest rattling bones, the venerable tones of the *Dies Irae* (a medieval hymn that can also be heard in Berlioz's *Symphonie Fantastique*), and a part for lead violin that's second to none. Decried at its premiere, it has since become a "popular" classic. There have been many visual adaptations, including a wonderful silent film (directed by Dudley Murphy [Visual Symphony Productions, 1922]). The opening credits feature figures from those old woodblock prints, which animate slightly to form the title (predating Disney's *The Skeleton Dance* in 1929). In this film, set during an outbreak of the plague, personifications of Love and Youth dance to Death's tune.

Although Cazalis's poem contains no overt romantic element, a number of macabre poems from the eighteenth century most certainly do, including Gottfried Burger's *Lenore* (1773; famously quoted in *Dracula*) and *Der Tod und das Mädchen* (*Death and the Maiden*) by Mattias Claudius (1774), which underwent its own musical adaptation at the hands of Franz Schubert. In this piece we have once again a dialogue between Death and its intended victim. But although the medieval Death had no lady or mistress, here Death presents itself as a friend and cajoles the maiden into granting it her hand.

Keeping this image in mind, let us jump once again to the twentieth century and further, past the 1920s to the decade of *Beetlejuice* and *The Meaning of Life* (with *Bill and Ted's Bogus Journey* coming only slightly thereafter). Here we discover the dead dancing to a rather different tune, one that was delivered to audiences with its own, intrinsic visuals—Michael Jackson's *Thriller.*

> Night creatures callin'
>
> The dead start to walk in their masquerade
>
> There's no escaping the jaws of the alien this time
>
> (They're open wide)
>
> This is the end of your life . . .

The full film (directed by John Landis [Optimum Productions, 1983]) depicts the popular singer as a teenager who has taken his appalled date to a horror film. When she flees the theatre, he follows, singing the song and gradually winning her over. Walking hand in hand, they pass a graveyard from which the dead begin to rise, presumably in response to the voice of horror icon Vincent Price. When the couple are surrounded, Jackson metamorphoses into a bony but still fleshed-out figure and leads the dead in a frenetic dance.

Is this a danse macabre in anything even resembling the medieval sense? The decaying aspects of the dead do suggest a variety of life stages and social positions: there is a business suit and tie, a white bridal ensemble, a glitzy disco outfit, and one man in shirt-sleeves and braces. It is hard to escape the conclusion that, like Claudius's *Der Tod,* Jackson has led this young and beautiful girl out to join them. Unlike her eighteenth-century counterpart, however, she declines, fleeing to the dubious shelter of a nearby house. Slighted, the dead pursue her. As they finally break through the door, she appears to wake from a nightmare and Jackson, who has resumed his living appearance, says he will take her home. But his last glance back at the camera leaves no doubt that any idea of escape is an illusion. In this, at least, the form holds true.

Let us jump another two decades. In 2005, the Masters of Horror television series combined directors and authors of classic horror to produce new hour-long projects. Episode 3 was Richard Christian Matheson's "Dance of the Dead" (directed by Tobe Hooper [IDT Entertainment]). It too depicts the dead dancing. But these corpses are the victims of a drug that preserves the body's basic motor functions after death. They are collected by an unscrupulous nightclub owner who makes them "dance" for his clientele. Jackson at least cajoled his victim, but there is no persuasion here, no offer of comfort. There is an element of judgement, in the decision made by the protagonist with respect to her sister's remains, but nothing like Holbein's reforming fury.

The fact is, today's popular culture features animate corpses aplenty. From Lydia's favourite *Night of the Living Dead* (written by John A. Russo, directed by George Romero [Image Ten et al., 1968]—which *Thriller's* house sequence overtly glosses), onward to the present night, they have been shambling out of every graveyard in ever-increasing numbers, with no purpose but to reduce the living to their own state. What may we read from this? It strikes me that there is something significant, even sobering, in the fact that the majority of our moving corpses hunt and kill instead of dance or warn. Whether it plays out that way or not, the living in these narratives always believe there is a way to escape, or that death can be shot between the eyes.

Neil Gaiman provides a charming alternative in *The Graveyard Book* (HarperCollins, 2008). The gist of this tale is an orphaned child who stumbles into a graveyard and is adopted by the ghostly inhabitants. In the course of many strange adventures, it turns out this is by no means the only time the dead and living have interacted in Old Town. Once every eighty years, when the winter ivy blooms, the living inhabitants and the dead of its graveyard come together in a joyous dance, which only the dead remember fully the next day. The living adumbrate the experience into symbol and moral, and those few who have already experienced this dance greet the procession from the graveyard with calm acceptance:

> Gracious lady, this I pray,
>
> Join me in the Macabray.

This too is a *memento mori*. Every society finds its own way of dealing with, of articulating death, and a macabre curiosity can be expressed in many ways, including the idea, glossed from Claudius, noted by Jackson, of accepting an invitation. But this is a danse that demands, not sheets or cowls, but one's best and most festive clothing. It comes with flowers that the dancers give their partners in recognition of their shared, ultimately human nature. Above all, Gaiman's danse is, like that of Jean Le Fevre, not an irrevocable commitment. It may be joined temporarily, then abandoned, and then taken up again, as the participant's need dictates. It may not, in the end, be avoided, but there is still something to be said for being polite.

In summary, the danse macabre appears to be one of those rare images thrown up by human experience, the resonance of which lingers long after the original circumstances have passed (choreomania has not been medically recognised since the mid-seventeenth century, although witnesses to modern raves might disagree). Although not as well known or as widely disseminated as the grim reaper or the ghost, it nonetheless has currency. Even lacking any knowledge of its antecedents, most people in contemporary Western culture correctly interpret a danse macabre when one turns up, however fragmented—the video clip for the Chemical Brothers' song "Hey Boy, Hey Girl" (1999; directed by Nic Goffey and Dominic Hawley) comes to mind. When skeletons start break-dancing, we get the point. And in that moment, no matter how polite the invitation or flippant the presentation, we may well feel a disturbance, concerned with or causing a fear of death.

Bibliography

Aries, Phillipe. *The Hour of Our Death*. Trans. Helen Weaver. London, United Kingdom: Penguin, 1977 (rpt. 1981).

Arnold, Catharine. *Necropolis: London and Its Dead*. New York, New York: Simon and Schuster, 2006.

Barber, Paul. *Vampires, Burial and Death: Folklore and Reality*. New Haven, Connecticut: Yale University Press, 1988.

Browning, Robert, ed. *German Poetry from 1750 to 1900*. New York, New York: Continuum, 1984.

Chaucer, Geoffrey. *The Canterbury Tales*. Trans. Nevill Coghill. London, United Kingdom: Penguin, 1951 (rpt. 1987).

Frayling, Christopher. *Vampyrs, Lord Byron to Count Dracula*. London, United Kingdom: Faber and Faber, 1991.

Hagstrøm, Martin. *The Medieval Dance of Death*, www.dodedans. com/Eindex.htm

Hecker, J. F. C. *The Black Death and the Dancing Mania*. Trans. B. G. Babbington. London, United Kingdom: Cassell, 1888.

Huizinga, Johan. *The Waning of the Middle Ages.* 1924. Trans. F. Hopman. London, United Kingdom: Penguin Books, 1990.

Lecouteux, Claude. *The Return of the Dead: Ghosts, Ancestors, and the Transparent Veil of the Pagan Mind.* 1996. Trans. Jon E. Graham. Toronto, Canada: Inner Traditions International, 2009.

Platt, Colin. *King Death: The Black Death and Its Aftermath in Late-Medieval England.* London, United Kingdom: UCL Press, 1996.

Polack, Gillian, and Katrin Kania. *The Middle Ages Unlocked: A Guide to Life in Medieval England, 1050–1300.* Stroud, United Kingdom: Amberly Publishing, 2015.

Richardson, Ruth. "The Corpse and Popular Culture." In *The Body: Death, Dissection and the Destitute.* Chicago, Illinois: University of Chicago Press, 1987.

Sadie, Stanley, ed. *The New Grove Dictionary of Music and Musicians.* London, United Kingdom: Macmillan, 1980.

LITTLE DEATHS

Boat of a Million Years

All aboard the funeral barque!

Tonight we sail from west to east

along re-stau, the passage from the tomb.

Anubis at the prow, gods at the oars,

sliding along a serpent's back.

The mourners kneel, with ash upon their heads,

harp and drum set ready on the deck.

Offerings at the base of the mast,

of bread and beer; our rations for a journey

that lasts a million years.

In the cabin, a golden leopard bears

a dead woman on its back.

A dead falcon, wrapped in new linen.

O! how far this boat must go!

And always return

to the mountains of Akhet.

Cast off! Cast off!

What a darkness this is, what a night,

without stars.

The coffin holds the stars,

as it holds all of creation,

bound in a dead woman.

Her groin the moon, her breast the sun,

her face a mirror reflecting all that is.

The Tomb Robber's Complaint

I went to the tombs in the west of Nō,
With my chisel of copper in my hand,
And entered the realm of the ones below,
With my chisel of copper in my hand,
And there I beheld all the images dread,
By the light of a barely burning brand,
Of scorpion, snake, and the beetle-head,
As the ashes collapsed upon my hand.

I opened the door with the jackal seal,
With my chisel of copper in my hand.
Glints in the dark did a treasure reveal,
And I took up the metal in my hand.
Amongst all the jewels that the casket bore
Was a scarab with gilding very grand.
I'd stolen it twice from the tombs before!
But I reached out and took it in my hand.

The priest may pronounce and the mayor may roar,
With the rod of his office in his hand;
A market takes place on the eastern shore
When the sun boat departs the double land,
Where fine statuette and the beard of Ptah—
Which the pious had placed beneath the sand—
With names all erased only cost a jar,
From a man with a burn upon his hand.

*   *   *

By day I labour in the temple grounds,
With my chisel of copper in my hand.
Behold the high priestess commence her rounds
With a vessel of copper in her hand.
She is such a one as the gods adore,
Who the truth of the world may understand;
I wish my adventures had shown me more
Than a fiend carven by an ancient hand.

That the dark had deigned to pronounce my name,
As I stood with my chisel in my hand,
And cried to Osiris the act was shame,
As I stood with my chisel in my hand.
That serpents out of the walls would rear,
Though the terror undo me where I stand,
The corpse might descend from its golden bier
And would offer, then, to take me by the hand.

Vanth—A Myth Derived

Vanth

is a name carved in an Etruscan tomb,

a bronze woman whose arms are wreathed in snakes,

the beating of rainbow-shaded wings,

the stranger at the banquet,

a torchbearer in dark places

who comes to announce the end.

That's what we know, from statue, vase, and wall.

The Etruscans did not write her story down

in any way that we may read today.

For all we know

it's right there in the *Liber Agramensis*.

But lacking a key to the Etruscan script,

I asked the darkness.

I sat in darkness, pondering Etruscan tombs,

their phosphorescence and porous passageways,

and this is how the dark replied.

Vanth

is a huntress without peer,

the strong-limbed daughter of a wealthy house,

whose delight lies in scaling rocky crags

and stalking the Ciminian Forest;

tireless in pursuit of the wounded beast,

her blade stops the pain.

The scholarship agrees,

citing her kilt and furry boots in the tomb of the Anina.

Her breasts are bare. A symbol of abundance

and charity, before the rise of Rome.

Etruscan women enjoyed a freedom

in all things, and furthermore

my vision grants to her a little boy

to follow in her steps, to hold her spear,

and clean the spoils.

Now I see a feast.

A very grand occasion: there are fresh rushes

and purple hangings in the hall.

Etruscans loved their feasts

and this will be a special one indeed,

with saffron cakes and wine set out in bowls.

For whether she is widow now disposed

to love again, or took her lover young,

before his passage to the state of man,

tonight shall see their rite.

Vanth for her part vows

that she alone will bring meat to the table,

to spare her father's herds and prove

herself the equal of her fame, and as a gift.

A bounteous gift to him that she shall wed.

So sets out in her boots, with hair tied back.

The boy comes on behind and leads the mule.

Soon both are laden with wild sheep of the crags

and deer of the forest,

the Ciminian Forest whose trees are as old as the world.

Most of all, she seeks a fattened boar.

Vanth

is a slight crunching of the fallen acorns,

a side-step as the bristle-back charges,

a bronze barb sunk deep into the flesh.

Rejoicing in the squeal and rush,

then tracking the thin trail of blood

deep into the shadowed gully.

The boar's trail leads to a cave.

Here baulk her companions, beast and boy.

They will not enter the mouth of the underworld.

Aita's mouth, with its mossy lips

and grey and nubby teeth, his tongue a snake.

His sour breath cascades across them all.

The mountain crest, an oracle's conic cap.

Vanth tells the boy to wait, then lights her torch

and ventures in.

The snake hisses a bane: she picks it up

and tells it she is stalking wounded prey.

It finds itself unable to protest.

Batting aside the shades who rise

to drink at the scarlet trickle, she goes down,

down, ever down,

and comes at last to the tenebral chasm

where stands Charun,

Aita's doorman

and escort of such dead as need encouragement

to walk the lonely path.

In the tomb of the Anina, Charun stands with Vanth,

two figments flanking the eternal door,

as if to say there are two ways to do this

and one involves a maul.

In all representations, hair bristles from his skin,

his face contorted by tusk and heavy brow,

muscled and squat, a horror to behold.

Speaks Vanth:

"To change your shape is a good trick,

but I'm not fooled. The blood leads here.

I know a boar when I see one."

The struggle is fierce, as one might expect.

But it has been an age

since anybody laid a hand on Charun,

let alone a bronze-skinned woman.

Catching his hammer in her net,

she trips him with her spear

and sends him sprawling, weapon out of reach.

She binds him hand and foot, and maybe he

does not resist her quite the way he ought.

This is the sin.

For, hauled into the light across her shoulders,

he is helpless
and the golden world begins to shake.
Water from the shady stream recoils
while birds burrow into loam,
for the natural course of death has been reversed.

Vanth
is striking down the aged, white-haired ram,
pinning the ewes to their seats with darts,
culling the screaming lambs
and slitting the throat of the golden deer
whose beauty tears her heart,
robed as she is, from head to foot, in richest crimson.

Then she turns to the terrified boy
in the ruin of his home, the corpses of his kin,
and says, "Here lie the spoils.
Wash and gut them as I taught you
and rub them well with spice against the flies.
Then build up the fire. Soon the feast begins."

What other form could her madness take?
Whether a simple consequence of her return
from darkness or Aita's ploy
to rescue Charun, who is suitably contrite.
The spectre of a thousand battlefields
brought low by a huntress, armed with net and spear!
The law of death defied in pursuit of a boar!
The dread lord

can only think that there is talent here.

He offers Vanth her wings

and she accepts. Somewhere beneath the blood

she knows what she has done

and there is no way back.

Aita twines his snakes about her arms,

exchanging both her weapons for his sword

and scroll on which is written mortal fate.

Returns to her the torch

that now gives off no earthly gleam.

Henceforth she will hunt for him alone

and people come to pray;

it will be Vanth who finds them in the end,

for she is beautiful to see

and never lets the suffering drag on.

What of her son?
Abandoned in a mansion of the dead?
The boy
is inaugurating funeral rites,
performing both the meanest task and the most sacred,
pariah and priest in ages yet to come,
a black tunic on the twilit streets of Rome,
a black hat in London bound with fog;
and even today,
his descendants labour beneath the shadow of wings.

Libitina's Garden

I. THE GROVE

No temple stands within the walls of Rome
to her who is Dis Pater's palatine.
The cypress branch outside the shuttered home
denotes a grove beyond the Esquiline
where ash sequesters souvenirs of dread—
the greater bones may well resist the flame—
and all the earth is rancid with such dead
as left the future neither wealth nor name.
Her votaries both winged and fanged compete
with witches for the choicest scavenging.
The foulest odours mingle with the sweet
of spices flung in hasty offering.
No image of her overlooks this place,
yet all who die will recognise her face.

II. VESPILLONIS

Divine Fortuna wars with ancient Nox.
By day, the portal Esquiline is barred
to all who might be judged unorthodox,
but darkness strips great Rome of its façade,
erasing privilege in the cobbled street,
as those whose sandals leave a smear of ash
rouse terror by the shuffle of their feet

surpassing both the prison and the lash.

For every corpse, regardless of its name,

departs the city under Nox's eyes.

The stretcher bearers handle all the same,

though mime and flambeaux offer a disguise.

But let her blink: a star comes tumbling down.

Dread Libitina stalks towards the crown.

III. The Dream of Augustus

Still mortal, the new Emperor awakes

within his silken sanctum, sure of threat.

The watch lamp gleams, no shout the silence breaks,

but through the drapes he spies a silhouette

bespeaking woman with averted face,

a stubbled scalp and shoulder curving bare.

At once a presence and an empty space:

words fall like ashes, sifting through the air.

"If you would have Rome prosper, see you grant

a fair and wholesome prospect to the dead.

Enriched with stone and every fragrant plant

the world bestows, lest fever turn my head."

Then all fell dark: arising terror-tasked,

Augustus did all that the goddess asked.

Buried in Jade

For the Princess Tou Wan

The meditation of jade
commences with a single square.
Can you picture it? Hold within your mind
the three dimensions, approaching thus the fourth?
Consider its proportions, each to each,
how stable and harmonious the whole.
Now contemplate its smoothness,
near frictionless,
this tear-drop slips through time.
The moon's tears,
condensed on earth in green.
Leaf green.
Snow green.
The green of deep wells.
How things ephemeral are here preserved.
And once you grasp this paradox,
and once this square exists for you
as item as in kind,
place it above the spirit well that opens in the chest.
Envisage, now, the next.

Bind them together with gold threads of your will.
So may conviction spread
across the fret of being, chest to crown
and stomach down to stem; the paths through which
the vital essence flows.

The torso cased in jade, a casket now
befitting holy sutras.
The limbs are wrapped in jade, each fingertip
becomes a dragon's claw.
The head bears jade like scales, and so
the face becomes the moon.
Distant, yet all-seeing.
Suited more for worship than for love,
with nothing left to kiss.

So you may pass through darkness,
through the hours of stone and silence,
essential nature cycling ever
pure and pristine.
Through the shroud of forgetting and the sealing of the world.
Through the stretching of hours into years,
and years into ages;
a timeless thing.
But should this prospect please you,
then beware.
Take care not to sustain the rote
beyond most urgent need.
For fear that, when the light returns,
as one day it shall do,
there stands a hollow chamber
strewn with memories and dust.
A cold pillow,
an emptied name,
and a scattering of squares in the shape of something once alive.

The Stone of Sacrifice

You may well wonder how the stone survived.
Wasn't it destroyed? Wasn't it cast down
when soldiers sanctified by shot and steel
arrived to slaughter its red-handed priests
and sacked their city, melted down their gold?
And how could it endure the missionaries
that raised their cross upon the temple steps?
Then followed the accretion of clay brick,
of roads and rails, and concrete at the last.

But you can tell it's real, even through glass.
This complex of conditioned air and light
is fashioned to preserve and yet display.
Secure, it glows like embers, like a jewel.
Yet to the first who dared the scoriac peaks,
it was much more. To come upon a plug
of crimson midst the black obsidian!
The Gods had made the world from their own blood
and these men had the wit to know a scab.

They gave their blood to carve it. Water, sand,
and wooden drills propelled by human hand
created faces: yes, those things are faces.
The numinous equipped with teeth and tongue.
And yet, it was the natural shape of stone
that gave the rite. And now you feel surprise

that it should be so small. The surgeon's slide
and mortuary slab inform your thoughts:
this is no bed. A prop beneath the back.
To kneel and lean, and show, is no despite:
it is a gift. Surrendering this way
the warrior returns to infancy.
Priests held them down, but did you know they spoke?
For priest and victim shared the potent draught,
receiving visions of the world to come.
The victim's words were hearkened over all,
for he gazed upwards to the sovereign sun.
The priest gazed down. Through skin and ribs, into
the ever-beating heart within all things.

How many died upon this whorl of rock?
The legends say that twenty thousand men
gave up their lives when first the stone was set.
And thence the sacred year progressed serene
a hundred times, from planting to the pick.
Each season duly paid in mortal blood
to granting sky and all-embracing earth.
And this was known: the missionaries took
confession of their captives, heard their songs
and saw the figures carved upon the walls;
recorded all, so their achievement might
be measured by the horror overcome
so deftly. How then did the stone survive?
An adept would already know the truth.

They must have laughed, the faithful that remained,
to hear the new God asked no sacrifice:
that blood was not the germ of this new world.
Twelve times the dedication was surpassed
as soldiers slew and plague raged through the streets—
a sacrifice of unimagined zeal!
The stone, not broken but buried by the new,
by duelling ground, the gallows tree and gaol;
the stone, rejoined to earth, accepted these
new rites, and over time the Gods drank deep.
Adjusted to a hectic calendar
where sacrifice could come at any time.
Came to accept exchange of weak for strong,
impure for perfect. So the stone endured;
became, unseen, foundation of a state.
Until the day it saw the light once more:
an accident, they say, while laying wire.

And do you think they stripped the stains away,
when first they placed it on its rubber bed?
And now they ship it off to foreign shores:
they say this tour encompasses the world.
A gesture of goodwill, of cultural pride,
a nation claiming space upon that stage
where each competes in curiosities.
A round stone, carved with angular grotesques
and glyphs no one can read. That draws your eye,
your steps across the floor. You know it's real

and whether you believe my tale, or no,
you can't deny that there is power here.
Perhaps there is, you say. But no one now
shall feed the Gods. There's nowhere left today
where people make a rite of murdering,
inventing crimes to so condemn their own,
permit hot blood to saturate the ground,
send smoke into the sky and claim it good.
So you may say; I shake my head and smile,
and ask how you can possibly think that.

Dual Purpose

A lantern casts a shadow in the day,
and little things of darkness fight for room,
where iron fretwork turns the sun away,
and bull's eye panels cast a spectral bloom.
Such demons as are sloughed like ash from Hell,
and lost familiars, waiting witch's prayer.
Glimpse fledgling gargoyles, yet to grow a shell,
and spirits trapped in necromantic snare.
As men may huddle in a shaft of light,
as twilight drowns the square and meeting hall,
so many of the haunts that give them fright,
cling writhing there, until the night shall fall.
And when the glass at last begins to heat,
a wave of terror rushes up the street.

Revenants of the Antipodes

Each sunset, now inverted Autumn lies
as red and cold as murder on the fields,
the hoary squatter rides the bleeding trails.
His shapeless hat hides eyes like empty pits,
or so they say: his ancient duster sags
like blowfly strike across his horse's rump.
No dog for years, yet into night he rides,
beneath the old wind pump's abscissional blades.

His cornstalks rattle bare, his vines crawl dead
to lever up the shingles on his hut.
His pumpkins seek the creek: his sheep, god knows.
He hunts, these nights. With scythe across his back
he seeks to kill the things that took his wife.
Not men, he swore, when you could read her name,
"Meine liebling," carved upon the wooden board.
There is a mason now, we box our dead
and fence the headstones in. Yet he believes
in revenants that once possessed this land,
the charcoal ghosts of those his kind displaced,
who mingle their stick bodies with the trees,
who spread their twiggy fingers in the fields
to waste the crops and take the cattle's strength,
build honeycomb inside a woman's womb.

*　　*　　*

Such things as these must be severely curbed,
and broken, staked and burned, before they cease.
His forebears taught him, in another place.
And who would argue? Every night we see
this figure lurk in graveyard, field, and at
the edge of town. This dusty spectre of
what used to be. Now that the church is roofed,
the pavement laid, and railway drawing near,
they say a child went missing in the dusk
and cattle have been found with tendons slashed.
The creek runs black and foul: it seems like time,
past time, indeed, to turn his dust to ash.

Mourning Rites

If I should keep a lock of hair
wound tight within a cameo,
what should you think but I compare
all suitors to one lost below?
You would console me as I grieve,
not dreaming that I might believe
you culpable. Why should you care
what weird this token may bestow?

If I should keep a candle lit
beside an image of the dead,
perhaps you will not welcome it
as chaperone, the painted head
of one betrayed. But etiquette
demands that you be patient yet.
Not questioning if this be fit,
nor why the candle should be red.

And though I wear a mourning dress
of metal lace and bombazine,
you brush, with seeming carelessness,
against my arm, your fingers keen
to venture more. But should a scratch,
as pin might make or cufflink catch,
appear, how could you ever guess
what ceding me those drops would mean?

And should the dead invade your sleep
and drag you to your judgement night,
be sure I will your vigil keep
with all solemnity that might
become the necromantic art.
To flay your soul and stop your heart
is mine. And though the price be steep,
revenge is lover's sacred right.

The Necromancer's Question

Did you think to escape me by this ploy?
To escape *me?* Did you think you could hide
so I would not in season find you out?
And dig yourself so deep into this grave
that I could not exhume you, should I choose?
I must call this a poor and common plot
for such as you, and an unworthy death.
I see it now, and scarce can bear the thought!
To break yourself upon the mundane wheel,
to suffocate so slowly, day by day
beneath the weight of earth, who gleamed so bright,
who saw so clear and far! And did you think
that as all darkened, so you would forget?
By subtle transfer, I too would forget?

A common grave, and yet it has some charm;
An avenue of solemn, shading trees,
now lit by lamps as darkness claims the sky.
Such quiet neighbours, such a spread of grass.
White roses at your head, brick at your feet.
But false the name engraved upon the post;
I know the truth, and now I see that here
you swelled, engendered small and squirming things;
To share your bed with such profligacy!
But yes, I understand your real intent,
to gain annihilation through decay.

But we were strong, my friend, who taught me love.
The magic that we wrought was stronger yet.
Those sigils in your skin protect you still:
your form is whole, your eyes, they are aware.

You knew full well that I would not forget.
Not in a thousand years; such is the price
of this my Art, the sweet, forbidden Art
that once we shared. I bring dreams into light,
distil desire. On summoned wings, I fly—
oh, how we flew! How sang, how wonderful
were you and I! And even in your sleep
that memory struck, and so your rising gas
became blue flame. And so it was that on
this late Midsummer's Eve, I found you out.
You stirred to feel my tread upon the grass.
Then heard my voice command your corpse to rise,
by your true name. Remembered then, too late,
the dead no longer have recourse to flight.

But now, my slave, you must recall my touch.
The coldness of your skin gives me no pause.
As my hands play your nerves awake, my breath
shall resurrect your lungs, my kiss your heart.
Of greater value than black pearls in wine,
this kiss, and of more potency. And now,
as muscles twitch and tongue begins to stir,
I conjure you to speak, and not to lie.

This sovereign Art interrogates the dead
and such you are: your choice was made long since.
You abdicated wand and word, and fled,
left me upon the crossroads, crimson-stained.
Did you think that would weaken me? Destroy
the tang of my sharp will? Not for one day.
Else you would not have taken such long steps.

I cherished deep those stains upon my hands,
inscribing sign and sigil in that ink.
So vast our sanctum seemed, but I kept faith.
Through cobwebbed noon and midnight's blackened vault,
the lonely hours saw me attend the flame.
I starved and stole; performed such sacrifice
as made the one you saw seem but a game.
And now you claim that was the way you died!
That mine own blade had entered in your heart.
Whatever you believe, the fear was all:
your fear of what I dared. Had I not laughed—
but how may I say now that you were wrong?
How may I swear that you alone were safe?
How may I even wish that you had stayed?
And there it is. The knowledge that I craved,
Not from your tongue at all, but from my own.

Left in the shell of our vast sanctum, there
I tended well the flame, annealed my will,
so grew in solitude, in power and time

to fill it. Now my name elicits awe.
My slightest work commands a fitting price.
I have attained all once we dreamed, and more;
such wisdom as could only come with time.
The truth that at the crossroads was unguessed.
And not one part of this may I regret.
Perhaps, if you had stayed, we would have done
the like, but not the same in part or whole.
So do I owe you thanks? Nor payment, no.
To leave was your own choice. This one is mine.

So on your brow I lay my final kiss,
complete the work that neither could alone.
Return you to your bed and at each step
let first the borrowed fire vacate your eyes—
Dark gods, your eyes! I'd keep them so for aye,
as mirror or preserved within a ring.
But I am done, so let them cloud once more,
and let your hair grow thin and grey, and fall,
your sinews slacken and your belly burst,
and even those ink vows beneath your skin
must drain away, must drain into the dark
where all things coalesce, save you and I.
Peace shall return to this sepulchral green.
And yet I think that you will not rest well.
The silence once resumed, will not rest well.
I think at each All Hallows, you will stir.

Tattered Livery

A paradox awaits their eyes:
a courtier in beggar's guise!
A ragged, jagged, mad array
and yet suggestive of the day
when I, perhaps, was much like *them*.
A most ingenious stratagem!
For many holding this belief
will offer tokens of relief
to turn their own ill luck aside.
What fallacy, what foolish pride
left this young fellow so bereaved?
But in this, they are all deceived.
There is a glory in my dress
surpassing all they might possess!
There is a river, dark and strong,
that carries all who dream along
and, drifting, I could not resist
a pale meander, thick with mist,
so found the lake that never can
reflect the face of star or man.
Instead, the captive of the stream
beholds the phosphorescent gleam
of sunken, lost and ruined things
enshrouded by their sails and wings,
and floating hair. As life recedes,
flavescent, a corona bleeds

from all who die in hate and fear,
and all in time are gathered here
where he who lifts his gaze will see
black towers rising endlessly.
In bravery, catastrophe!
And he who grants me charity
dips hand into the river, he
will feel it cold and shivery,
I wear my tattered livery
and serve a tattered king.

A branch the drowning man reprieves:
a tree with needles for its leaves
and lightest touch of naked skin
conducts these slivers deep within.
Beside this tree, the stairs of stone
admit such supplicants alone.
A thousand steps, eroded by
a thousand, thousand such as I.
A thousand steps above the falls
to enter the tenebral halls
wherein the ever-moving feast
leaves ashes strewn and platters greased,
and there the prints, in ichor sweet,
of hooves and claws, and dancing feet.
The catch of laughter, trill of strings,
the raucous echoes screaming brings:
so he may wander, night on night

before he sees the fulvous light,
before he hears the silken voice
and understands how every choice
was none at all: no prize to gain,
the wearisome annular chain
has brought him here, already bound,
a fitting task already found.
To see one's soul turn crystalline
within that hand, and so resign!
To see it join the lucent drape
of all who in this way escape
the ache of their autonomy,
suspended for eternity.
In slavery lies ecstasy!
And all who lay their hands on me
suspecting fraud or thievery,
by proxy touch the sliver-tree!
I wear my tattered livery
and serve a tattered king.

And as the pangs of day replace
the shrilling pipe and barbed embrace,
I tread through streets no longer known,
for all their former sense has flown.
These soaring spires and tiny greens!
Whole lives compacted into screens!
I seek out those I knew before
and mark the Sign above their door:

the ones who scorned, the ones who stole,

and these His hunger swallows whole.

But one remains whose love was true,

I seek her out and peering through

a winter crevice, see her stand

before an easel, brush in hand.

Remember that *I* once stood there,

before the doubt, before despair,

before I knelt before the throne,

had visions that were all my own.

Believed it was my task to show

the world to all who did not know

the precious piece of cosmic art

of which they are themselves a part!

So vulnerable she seems, and slight,

and yet before her inner light

I am a mummy: gutted, dried,

with only darkness left inside.

But I do not resent the time

she has to draw and dance, and rhyme.

I watch and wait, until I see

the world reward its devotee

with poverty and mockery!

And when she reaches out to me,

my darkness I shall give her free;

her deepest heart a-quiver, she

shall share this tattered livery

and love our tattered king.

Don't Open the Box!

I tell you, don't open the box
with the latch and the leonine claws.
Don't mind what's inside it: if I choose to hide it,
it's surely no business of yours.
To cross me in this would be pointless,
if temptingly unorthodox.
I know it's intriguing, but it's so fatiguing
for me to keep watch on this box . . .

That—*swear*—you won't open the box
and we'll both get along with our day.
You might try spelunking, perhaps apple-dunking,
or else a few rounds of croquet.
It's really no kind of a challenge,
if I'm not around to outfox.
So long as you think it some valueless trinket,
then why would you open the box?

Oh, *why* did you open the box?
Did you have to go play the explorer?
Did you think it was Christmas, or maybe that this was
Olympus and you were Pandora?
And now you have seen what's inside it,
your punishment will be approx-
imate to the cause: we both know that it was the
last person to open the box!

THE LOQUACIOUS CADAVER

a fable

METRO POLICE
?

One night in the ghastly adolescence of the world, when men and women had learned enough to be sure they knew everything but were yet to take responsibility for themselves, the Beetle found a corpse in the desert. The desert had become the barren stretch between cities, scarred with steel rails and cracked concrete, and the Beetle had not encountered such a thing in many years.

"A corpse," she clicked, "left for my tending. I will carry it away underground, so that it may transform and rise again."

"No," came a croaking and the Bird descended, flapping her black wings. "From high above I saw the human fall. I will bear it into the sky, so it may become a spirit."

"No," came a barking, and the Dog came running over the sand. "I tracked this human in dying, and now I shall take it to my master, who will judge its eternal fate."

The three ancient psychopomps sat and glared at one another, for as the desert had shrunk, opportunities to perform their sacred duties had become rare. But in the great cycles of existence, few problems are without precedent and such conflicts had been resolved before.

"At the very least," said the Beetle, "I will lay my eggs in its tongue."

"At the very least," said the Bird, "I will take its eyes."

"At the very least," said the Dog, "I will remove its hands and entrails."

At this, the corpse stirred and said, "Excuse me, but you will do no such thing. I'm waiting here for the police and would like to look my best when they arrive."

"Eek!" shrilled the Beetle. "Lie still! Lie still!"

"You must not move," scolded the Bird. "And corpses do not talk!"

"We talk," replied the corpse, "to coroners and detectives. I hope you appreciate the exception I'm making for you."

"Well, I don't see anyone else here," huffed the Dog, "nor smell anything but you."

"They'll come: the story doesn't start until they come."

"What story?"

"The detective story: don't you watch television? Now get off me, you nasty vermin! Shoo!"

"We understand," said the Beetle patiently, "you're expecting the priests of your God to come. But it all comes down to one of three—"

"Not priests, police!"

"Well, what will these police do when they get here?" asked the Bird.

"Examine me to determine my identity and the cause of death. Then they'll put me in a van and take me away."

"Well, no wonder corpses are so hard to find! What happens to you then?"

"If I was murdered, then there's the hunt for the killer and the trial: it will be in the papers and everyone will talk about it. If it was an accident, then not so much: still less if natural causes. But I get an obituary, that's the important thing."

"What happens then?"

"I'm taken to a room and burned."

"And?"

"And that's it," said the corpse.

"That's it?" the Dog frowned. "I don't understand."

"You become smoke," suggested the Bird. "You go up into the sky."

"You become ash," suggested the Beetle. "You go down into the earth."

"I become nothing and go nowhere: that's why the obituary is so important." The corpse settled back into its original position. "Now, if you'll kindly leave me be."

Faced with the corpse's insistence, the psychopomps retreated.

"Load of tripe," grumbled the Dog. "I mean, we *know* that's not what happens!"

"Yes, but it seems they've forgotten," said the Bird.

"Forgotten very rigorously," said the Beetle. "We may have to give them a little prod. But first we must wait."

So the three waited as the sun rose and brightened, then dimmed and sank, and the corpse reddened and swelled, then blackened and shrank and still no one came. At last they approached the corpse again.

"Look," began the Beetle. "We don't mean to be insensitive, but you've been here a long while now."

"It will be harder for the detectives," the corpse slurred. "But that will only make the story more interesting."

"No one's coming," the Dog said bluntly. "No one comes here except people like you."

This struck the corpse sombrely. "I don't suppose one of you could take a message into the city?"

"I don't see why you're so set on becoming nothing," said the Bird.

"It's the only way I can remain what I was," said the corpse. "You really won't go and find them?"

"No," replied the three in unison.

"Then I will," said the corpse and sat bolt upright, causing the Dog and Bird to scatter and flinging the Beetle across the sand. All the parts that had once held together inside it jostled and jangled, but with a mighty effort of will it contrived to stand.

Then across rails and over concrete, the corpse teetered and tottered but managed to keep moving towards the buildings that quickly rose around it. And all unnoticed, the Beetle rode on its shoulder, with the Dog trotting behind it and the Bird circling overhead. They accompanied the corpse down a long street where at first it drew only brief glances from such people as were too tired and poor to care. But as they continued, the glances grew longer and the people rich enough to scream and energetic enough to run, and finally the police arrived.

When the vans pulled up, the corpse waved and attempted to explain the situation, but they answered only with bullets. These failed to harm it, of course, but did nothing to improve its disposition. It took hold of a man by the shoulders and shook him, and a woman by the throat, but neither would listen. And so it raged, overturning the vans and bending the guns into pretzels.

Eventually, the corpse decided it must seek for its obituary by itself and so it sought out the streets it had known in life. But no one there recognised it, even among those were caught in corners and could not avoid looking in its face. So it attempted to visit a dentist and, after the dentist said she could not perform an X-ray because everything had come loose inside, to engage a private detective. But the private detective said he could not take its fingerprints because its fingers were already black, and besides, the corpse had lost its wallet. Everywhere it went, there was only screaming and running, and frantic excuses. At last it saw a newspaper containing its picture, and thought that its search was over. But when it read the article, all it described was a walking corpse terrorising the city.

It sat down on the steps of the city hall. "It's too late!" it exclaimed. "I'm not what I was any more. I've changed so much that even the story is new!"

"Actually," said the Beetle, "I'm afraid it's very old."

"A corpse leaving the desert and rejoining the living world is rare," said the Bird, "but not new."

"You'll never be nothing now," said the Dog.

"So I might as well go with one of you," said the corpse. "Or all of you: I don't care."

"I'm afraid," said the Beetle, "that's no longer an option."

"What do you mean? You were fighting over me before!"

"But you not only started talking, you got up and walked," said the Bird. "That puts you beyond our reach."

"But you're right here beside me!"

"Here the only thing we are is nasty vermin," said the Dog. "There really isn't anything we can do."

"But I only got up because of you!"

"I suppose that's true," said the Dog.

"Oh, dear," said the Bird. "Silly us."

"But don't despair," said the Beetle. "Eventually people will get used to you. They'll grow curious and begin to follow."

"And they'll give me my obituary?" cried the corpse.

"Not yours, precisely," said the Beetle, "but I'm sure it will do."

So the corpse got up and continued walking, but slowly, avoiding the crowded places. Night came, and day came, and still it kept walking, looking for someone who would listen.

The psychopomps went their way, hungry but content. For they were ancient indeed and had witnessed the founding of many religions. They knew that there is nothing like a walking, talking corpse to turn people's minds towards something rather than nothing and to go back into the desert, seeking wisdom.

Lucubration

a composition that smells of the lamp

A most perplexing paradox, to write
so late at night with such a light as this,
banishing darkness from the magic ring;
but day thoughts are not night thoughts, so this hiss
of warming gas and stink of burning dust
must be the very consecrated 'cense,
the silver inlay and the mighty name
that lets me press the demon with a slim,
unsure advantage. Is this but his play,
awaiting chance to reft my soul away?
Still I would summon darkness! That each door
and window, underside and crack extends
into the furthest reaches of the byss,
all that has been, may come to be and is.

It seems that I have stalked tenebral paths,
leaves pressing thick and bends obscuring sight.
Only the scent of cereus and of rose
to mark the way: the velvet brush of moss
and kiss of web assurance of retreat.
This is my victim's garden, well beyond
the outer wall yet feel I still no fear—
a mask and blade ensure my welcome here.
To move so swift, so silently and sure!
No thorn ensnares, no twig betrays my step;
the grace of darkness speeds me to our tryst
in empty passage, else his very bed.
No matter whose the coin that bought this death,

of all that call this rotting city home,
there shall be heat, a muffled scream and blood
sweet on my lips, for I am nothing more
than wolf or pard, or any other bane
they seek to keep beyond the palisade.
Close now, all unaware my prey awaits,
a turn, and through the shivering of fronds
and shattering of water, there is light.

I see them through the arches where they dance
gilded by harpsichord and violin,
silvered by laughter and flirtatious glance;
none look without. To them the world is all
a crystal ball that catches candlelight
and sends motes spinning, hand in tender hand.
In peacock satin, broidered and bejewelled,
their faces masked as panther, wolf or skull
and he, 'tis surely he who thus affects
assassin's black, a blatant mockery.
For I must never stray within the light,
the legendry of my cruel craft maintain,
no partner take, save in the dance of death;
this code enshrined, yet how may I refrain?
Why do I stalk these sightless alley-ways
but for a glimpse of life's rose aureole?
Why take their coin and venture in their sphere
if not to touch all that I was denied
when fate cast me upon the darker shore?

I dance upon a dagger every night!
Why should I not dance here amongst the crush
of hip and shoulder, lacing lip and thigh?
How could they tell my visage from their own?
So entered I, and soon the answer learned.
Such answer as permits the gods to laugh
Such grace I had as lay beyond the dance;
where others faltered, I descried the tune,
nor caught a foot, nor brushed a careless hand
in weavìng ever closer to my prey:
Oh laughing gods, unravel how it may
be grace itself that gave myself away?
Questions assail me, laughter closes ranks
and hems me in. I can see nothing past
the light but light permits them to discern
the deed undone and mark, it is for that
I die, beyond a hundred crimson crimes.
Now as my judges bring the rod and flame
I cry for darkness, prodigal in shame
and only dread the work that they now do
will leave life's final shackle on my wrist.
All I have been brought screaming down to this.

Thus I retreat, and seek throughout the vast
for certain sanctum and yet deeper dark.
It seems I have walked colonnades aside
of hornèd heads with women's breasts, and known
a man's face rise above a lion's paunch,

serpents and scarabae with human hands
and phalluses: I say, not all were stone.
Across the sands disguising all above,
devoutly, pilgrims trace an ancient path
from out the lesser shadows of the night,
down cunning stairs that lead to us below.
Echoing vaults as chill and black as death,
where barks of granite draw their cargo nigh,
and stone papyrus holds the heavens high.
Our oracle brings men with azure beards
and layered robes, redheads with pallid skin,
bronze men and black: with offerings of wood,
of iron and silver, ivory and salt,
the oil of whales and one thing more, for here
no circle holds the demon kind at bay.
The supplicants pass columns in the murk,
offering bodies to a winged embrace
and throats to kisses bringing such sweet pains
as only teeth permit and blood contains.
They come for knowledge: knowledge they shall find
in scented smoke that frees the untrained mind,
murmured by shades and hissed by coiling fiends,
and whispered from the lips of blessed things
that pass above them, stirring fragrant wind.
Whate'er they seek, be it the fate of kings,
the course of wars, felicity of brides,
or cure of plagues: the answer here abides.
Yet none of these shall ever find the lake

where lotus blossoms raise their scented heads
above black waters, warm and thick as blood.
None shall approach the greatest mystery,
the beating stone, the nigresence within
the inmost shrine, where only priests may go.
Only the chosen: all these paths are mine.

Yet still there is a thing that troubles me:
dogging my step and stinging in my eye.
Not ghost nor genius, yet it flits along
the colonnade, a disc both flat and fleet.
I fail to catch it: then as I pursue
I recognise intrusion from above.
Within the ceiling gleams a single hole
and through that hole there lies a shining world
of tincts known only through their dying fall,
of sounds and scents, of trees and fields of grain,
loud rivers flowing underneath a sky
where rides a god that shows himself to all.
I am of those who see without their eyes,
kept from the world to force the subtle sense:
And though I now imagine sight and sound
and quake within, I know my duty well.
With sleeve across my face, a fragile mask
I seek out proper servants for the task
of sealing up this breach of sanctity.
Had I but looked, perhaps I would have seen
the doom that was foretold us long ago

approaching now. Perhaps I could have been
the saviour of some shard, and wrought a fate
somehow less cruel, and kept our memory
intact for all the ages yet to come.
The dust sifts down, and yet I see it not.
The columns creak, yet I walk on until,
with booming shriek and rushing tide of sand,
the stony heavens split apart in flame
and men descend who seek no wisdom here.
The spirits shriek and yet they hear them not.
The monsters writhe but they can only see
statues adorned with gold and many gems
run molten in the furnace of the day.
All I might be is given to decay.

Once more, once more I flee into the dark
and, shrieking, seek out such a potent form
as may defend the fragments of my soul.
No weakness now, of either love or fear.
This blade I bear is forged of ancient shards.
This mask I wear was stolen from a tomb.
Armour I carry, and an evil name,
that Christian priests may use to conjure hate.
I am the wolf's right hand, the raven's throat,
who rises from the forests of the north
where endless run the trees whose blackened trunks
and gloomy branches scarify the sun
and men mistake the days for nights until

dread madness seize them, else they chance on me.
I come now from the necromantic groves
as crest of storm devouring the bright day,
and all the slaves in fields and cities quake:
their devil curse, that loosed me on the world.
Their devil, ha! They'd better blame their God.
Dreadful the sacrifice that has allowed
my conjuring, and it was not my hand
which spilled the blood across the altar stone.
In my ranks heretics and rebels crawl
who lost their lives upon the block or wheel,
and lovers slain for loving past the bounds,
proud pagans Roma never held in thrall,
the charcoal husks of witches, and yet more:
monsters and prodigies of form possessed
to make of man's perfection but a jest.
All share my hunger to extinguish light
and in this final victory to rest.

"O hear me now, you captives of the hour!
Yes, hear me now, you blind and shackled fools!
Prepare to welcome all you have despised.
The cross shall not avail you, nor the scourge.
Embrace us, love the grand catastrophe,
for by this turn or death, you shall be free!"
Walls crumble hissing into ancient sand
at my bare touch; the sputtering cannon dies
at merest glance, and where I tread the grass

is blackened and the earth gapes wide and births
yet more abominations at my call.
So die the knights, their armour but a glove
to animated tendrils of the dark;
So die the priests, their chastity consumed
by laughing nightmares, bringing bliss with fangs;
So die the mothers, shrieking out their right
to mercy to rough things of stone and clay
that never knew the pressure of the womb.
So die they all, and every child who cries.
The beacon fires, lanterns of the watch,
the flambeaux that illumine all the State,
the great cathedral seeming to contain
within a rose of glass the very sun,
now one by one, they die. All die and night
comes sweeping through the city like the tide,
the final flood that never shall recede.
One light remains within the highest tower,
one light alone, and this both faint and far,
but I'll not leave my vengeance incomplete.
My best companions running at my heels
and screeching in my wake, I take the stair
that circles ever upwards, ever on.
The light's a grin that mocks my every step!
The light's an eye that sees my deepest pain.
The light: the light is no more than a lamp
that casts a circle round a desk and chair,
and adumbrates the figure seated there

with pen in hand. And yet somehow in this
I see creation's round and all that is.

If I wrote in the darkness, the result
would be such scratchings and strange hieroglyphs
as any passing eye would think no more
than random marks, the proper work of flies
or imbeciles. If such the demon is,
my own self come to steel me to this task,
the greater soul of which I am the part
that weeps; my duty nonetheless is clear:
complete the work that is my purpose here.
As I return to darkness, so to light,
without whose hissing breath, I cannot write.

AFTERWORD

I have never read a book quite like this one. Kyla Lee Ward, building upon the promise of her first poetry collection, *The Land of Bad Dreams* (2011), has weaved together a compelling tapestry of poetry, fiction, and nonfiction, all unified by the theme of the *danse macabre* (the dance of death). Ward shows that this single theme is capable of infinite variety, and this book features a striking diversity of emotional resonance while nonetheless retaining a thematic and structural unity.

In the opening section, where Death holds a dialogue with a succession of hapless mortals who will all, in due course of time, come under his sway, Ward seems to channel the keen-edged wit and satire of Ambrose Bierce, who similarly saw in Death the ultimate arbiter of human destiny. But what is generally lacking in Bierce's work but present in Ward's is a sense of empathy with those human beings—whether high-born or low-born, rich or poor, successful or otherwise—who must all shuffle off this mortal coil when their time approaches. The dismal fate of the Office Worker, having spent a lifetime in futile busywork ("So many dreams, / all buried now, beneath the reams / of copying"), is etched in a few plangent lines.

The learned essay on the history of the *danse macabre* fittingly occupies a central place in this volume, leading to an array of longer poems that return in different ways to the book's overall theme. Whereas, in her essay, Ward explores the history of the *danse macabre* from its origins in the Middle Ages up to the present day (including some surprising appearances in contemporary films and song lyrics), the poems reach back much farther in time. The horrors of ancient Egypt ("Boat of a Million Years," "The Tomb Robber's Complaint") and Rome ("Libitina's Garden") are on display; and in "Vanth—A Myth Derived" Ward performs a tour de force in rooting her work in the culture of the Etruscans, that shadowy and obscure civilisation that preceded Rome on the Italian peninsula and were ultimately conquered by the latter. "Buried in Jade" evokes death in a Chinese setting.

Ward is at her best in such long poems as "The Necromancer's Question" and "Lucubration," the latter first published in a volume of poems inspired by two of the greatest weird poems in literary history, George Sterling's "A Wine of Wizardry" and Clark Ashton Smith's *The Hashish-Eater*. "Lucubration" is anything but a mechanical pastiche, its sonorous iambic pentameter lines echoing its impressive predecessors but reflecting Ward's own poetic sensibility. And we can hardly overlook "The Loquacious Cadaver," a vignette of succulent graveyard humour that shows Ward as deft in prose as in verse.

With each new work she produces, Kyla Lee Ward—who, like William Blake and Clark Ashton Smith, has chosen to illustrate her own work—makes clear why she should be regarded as one of the preeminent exemplars of contemporary weird poetry. *The Macabre Modern and Other Morbidities* is a book to be savoured unhurriedly and with due contemplation of its essential message: that Death is omnipresent and inescapable, and that its surface terrors may also hold some faint hope of relief for the weary creatures who will inexorably succumb to it.

—S. T. JOSHI

Some of this work has been published previously:

"The Danse Macabre" is adapted from the author's earlier essay on the topic in *Tabula Rasa* 2 (April 1994).

"Vanth—A Myth Derived." *Eternal Haunted Summer* (Summer Solstice, June 2017).

"Libitina's Garden—A Triptych." *Mythic Delirium* 4, no. 4 (April/June 2018).

"The Stone of Sacrifice." *Spectral Realms* 4 (Winter 2016).

"Dual Purpose." *Spectral Realms* 6 (Winter 2017).

"Revenants of the Antipodes." *HWA Poetry Showcase V*, edited by Stephanie Wytovich (Horror Writers Association, 2018). Winner of the 2018 Australian Shadows Award for poetry.

"Mourning Rites." *The Audient Void* 7 (2019).

"The Necromancer's Question." *Spectral Realms* 1 (Summer 2014) (as "Necromancy"). Reprinted in *The Year's Best Australian Fantasy and Horror 2014*, edited by Liz Gryb and Talie Helene. Perth, Western Australia: Ticonderoga Press, 2015.

"Tattered Livery." *Weirdbook* 37 (December 2017).

"The Loquacious Cadaver." *The Lion and the Aardvark: Aesop's Modern Fables*, edited by Robin D. Laws (London, United Kingdom: Stone Skin Press, 2012). Reprinted in *The Year's Best Australian Fantasy and Horror 2012*, edited by Liz Gryb and Talie Helene. Perth, Western Australia: Ticonderoga Press, 2013.

"Lucubration." *Avatars of Wizardry: Poetry Inspired by George Sterling's "A Wine of Wizardry" and Clark Ashton Smith's "The Hashish Eater,"* edited by Charles Lovecraft. Sydney, New South Wales: P'rea Press, 2012.

Kyla Lee Ward generally lives in Sydney, Australia, with her partner and sometime co-author David Carroll, a flerken (suspected) and a familiar (definitely). She has produced short fiction, articles, and poetry, including Stoker, Ditmar, Shadows, and Rhysling nominations, and won one-third of an Aurealis Award for the novel, *Prismatic* (co-written with David and Evan Paliatseas, and released under the name "Edwina Grey"). Her previous poetry collection, *The Land of Bad Dreams,* was released by P'rea Press in 2011 (rpt. 2016). An artist, actor (specialising in Grand Guignol and immersive theatre), and occasional playwright, she has travelled widely and rhymed adventurously, and researches when bored. Her boredom threshold is quite low, and thus her interests include swordplay, history, and occultism, as well as scaring innocent bystanders.

URL: www.kylaward.com Facebook: Kyla Ward

Gillian Polack is a writer and historian and has Ph.D.s in History and in Creative Writing. Several of her novels, one of her anthologies, and her monograph *History and Fiction* have been shortlisted for awards. She is a member of the group of historical fiction writers The History Girls and also of the author co-operative Book View Café.

URL: www.gillianpolack.com Facebook: Gillian Polack
Twitter: gillianpolack

S. T. Joshi is a widely published critic, editor, and fiction writer, and the author of *The Weird Tale* (1990), *I Am Providence: The Life and Times of H. P. Lovecraft* (2010), *Unutterable Horror: A History of Supernatural Fiction* (2012), and many other volumes. He co-edited (with Steven J. Mariconda) the historical anthology *Dreams of Fear: Poems of Terror and the Supernatural* (Hippocampus Press, 2013), and edits the weird poetry journal *Spectral Realms.*

The Macabre Modern and Other Morbidities by Kyla Lee Ward.
(August 2019)
ISBN: 978-0-9943901-3-4 (illustrated hardcover) $30AU
ISBN: 978-0-9943901-2-7 (illustrated paperback) $16AU
ISBN: 978-0-9943901-4-1 (illustrated ebook) $12AU

OTHER PUBLICATIONS FROM P'REA PRESS

Spores from Sharnoth and Other Madnesses by Leigh Blackmore.
(September 2008; rev. rpt. August 2010, May 2013, February 2016)
ISBN: 978-0-9804625-2-4 (paperback) $16AU

Emperors of Dreams: Some Notes on Weird Poetry by S. T. Joshi.
(November 2008)
ISBN: 978-0-9804625-3-1 (paperback) $15AU

Savage Menace and Other Poems by Richard L. Tierney.
(hardcover April 2010; paperback, ebook editions August 2019)
ISBN: 978-0-9804625-5-5 (illustrated numbered hardcover) $30AU
ISBN: 978-0-9943901-5-8 (illustrated paperback) $16AU
ISBN: 978-0-9804625-6-2 (illustrated ebook) $12AU

The Land of Bad Dreams by Kyla Lee Ward.
(September 2011; rpt. February 2016)
ISBN: 978-0-9804625-7-9 (illustrated paperback) $16AU

Avatars of Wizardry by George Sterling, Clark Ashton Smith, et al.
(November 2012; rpt. February 2016)
ISBN: 978-0-9804625-8-6 (illustrated paperback) $16AU
ISBN: 978-0-9804625-9-3 (illustrated ebook) $12AU

Dark Energies by Ann K. Schwader.
(August 2015; rpt. August 2015; February 2016)
ISBN: 978-0-9943901-0-3 (illustrated hardcover) $26AU
ISBN: 978-0-9804625-1-7 (illustrated paperback) $16AU
ISBN: 978-0-9943901-1-0 (illustrated ebook) $12AU

Publishes weird and fantastic poetry and nonfiction
c/-34 Osborne Road, Lane Cove,
NSW, Australia 2066
Website: www.preapress.com
Email: DannyL58@hotmail.com

P'REA PRESS